LITTLE BROWN BEAR
Does Not Want to Eat

Written by Claude Lebrun
Illustrated by Danièle Bour

Children's Press®
A Division of Grolier Publishing
New York   London   Hong Kong   Sydney
Danbury, Connecticut

"Little Brown Bear,"
says Papa Bear,
"finish eating
your food."

"I don't want
any more, Papa,"
he says.

"Little Brown Bear,
your food
is getting cold,"
says Papa.

"But Papa,
it doesn't taste good,"
says Little Brown Bear.

"And besides,
I'm not hungry."

"Eat one more
spoonful for Mama,"
says Papa,
"and one more
spoonful for me."

"All right, Papa,"
says Little Brown Bear.
"But then you must eat
one spoonful for me!"

This series was produced by Mijo Beccaria.

The illustrations were created by Danièle Bour.

The text was written by Claude Lebrun and edited by Pomme d'Api.

English translation by Children's Press.

Library of Congress Cataloging-in-Publication Data
Lebrun, Claude.
Little Brown Bear does not want to eat / by Claude Lebrun:
illustrated by Danièle Bour.
p. cm. — (Little Brown Bear books)
Summary: Little Brown Bear resists all the efforts to get him to eat his soup.
ISBN 0-516-07823-2 (School & Library Edition)
ISBN 0-516-17823-7 (Trade Edition)
ISBN 0-516-17803-2 (Boxed Set)
[1. Food habits — Fiction.] I. Bour, Danièle, ill. II. Title. III. Series: Lebrun, Claude.
Little Brown Bear books.

PZ7.L4698Ld
1996[E] — dc20
95-1134
CIP
AC